Special Delivery

Written and illustrated by Elliot Kruszynski

British Library Cataloguing-in-Publication data available.

ISBN: 978-1-908714-79-4

Published by:

Cicada Books Ltd
48 Burghley Road
London, NW5 1UE
www.cicadabooks.co.uk

Printed in Poland

Elliot Kruszynski is a London-based illustrator who enjoys spending time with his cat, Pablo, and having a GREAT time. His witty, colourful illustrations have featured on work for clients including Etsy and AirBnB. He is the illustrator of *Spot the Bot* (Laurence King 2019) and the author of two upcoming titles for Walker Books.

Special Delivery

elliot kruszynski

Today is an important day

because the
house is getting
a new baby!

Ding dong!
Special delivery!

Umm... hello, can I help you?

Hi, yes, I'm delivering a new baby to this address.

I'm sorry, there's been a mistake. That's not my brother.

No, no, I'm afraid I don't make mistakes.

This is the right house.

Bye bye.

Ding dong!
Special delivery!

Hello can I – Oh it's you!

Hi, yes, I'm
delivering a new baby
to this address.

I'm sorry, there's been a mistake. That's not my brother.

No, no, I'm afraid I don't make mistakes. This is the right house.

Bye bye.

Ding dong!
Special delivery!

You again?

Hello, yes, I'm delivering a new baby to this address.

But there's been a mistake, that's not my brother!

No, no, I'm afraid I don't make mistakes. This is the right house.

Bye bye.

Ding dong!
Special delivery!

What is it this time?!

Hello, I'm delivering a
new baby to this address.

But there's been a mistake!

No, no, I don't make mistakes.
This is the right house.

Bye bye.

Ding dong!
Special delivery!

Another one?!

Hello, yes, I'm delivering a new baby to this address.

But there's been a –

No, no, I'm afraid I don't make mistakes. This is the right house.

Bye bye.

Ding dong!
Special delivery!

Oh my...

Hi, I'm delivering a new baby to this address.

But –

No, no, I'm afraid I don't make mistakes. This is the right house.

Bye bye.

Ding dong!
Special delivery!

Hello again, yes
I know what
you are going
to say
but

I

don't

make

mistakes.

Ding dong!

Where's our baby?

Terrible.

Your deliveries are all in here!

Mum! Dad!

My little one!

Purrrr...

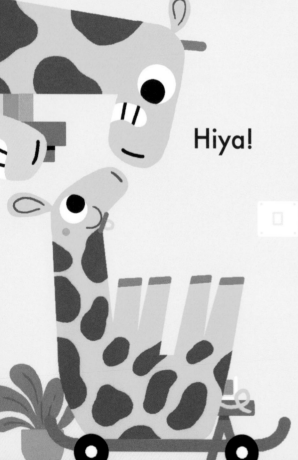

Hiya!

Ah, I almost forgot. There's just one last thing.

Would you mind signing here?

This one is an *extra* special delivery...